BUSTER

THE DOG WHO DANCED WITH DANGER

DAVEY J. ASHFIELD

COVER PAINTING BY KATE ASHFIELD

ILLUSTRATED BY TERRY GREENWELL

APS BOOKS

YORKSHIRE

APS Books,
The Stables Field Lane,
Aberford,
West Yorkshire,
LS25 3AE

APS Books is a subsidiary of the APS Publications imprint

www.andrewsparke.com

First published worldwide by APS Books in 2023

A catalogue record for this book is available from the British Library

FOR

KATE

CONTENTS

CHAPTER ONE
BUSTER GOES TO SCHOOL

"Buster, get off that sofa!"

Buster never moved his large head from the comfy sofa he was lying on. Slowly, he opened his big brown eyes to look pleadingly at his grandma. Despite her angry voice he stayed put on his very comfortable bed.

"That blooming dog!" his Grandad grumbled as he sat in his armchair shuffling his newspaper pages, glowering at the large brown dog. Buster dropped his head in between his paws hoping they would leave him alone.

"That dog never listens to me. He never follows the rules," his grandma cried out to her husband.

Buster looked at his grandma through his droopy eyes and wondered what on earth was wrong with her. *"I worry her head will explode,"* he thought. And then in his doggy brain he exclaimed, *"Oh no! Here she comes again."*

Before his red-faced grandma could reach him and give him a whack with her feather duster on his bottom, he slipped his legs off her precious new flowery sofa. The rest of his body followed very slowly, his sad eyes fixed on his tormentor. He lowered his back and legs and began to slink out of the lounge door.

He looked back pleadingly at his glowering grandad hoping he'd stop his crazy wife chasing him out of this lovely comfortable room. Unfortunately, for Buster the grumpy man just wacked him on his bottom with his newspaper. The poor dog jumped up and away from another wack and hurried out of the lounge and back to the safety of his own sofa in the kitchen.

"What on earth is wrong with me lying on that nice new comfy bed? All I want to do is be with them and talk to them. Why don't they understand that?" the tortured dog pondered as he crawled onto his very own old and torn, two seated sofa. He put his paws over his ears as his grandma slammed shut the kitchen door, locking him in his lonely prison cell.

"Will they never listen to me," he said to himself, as turned over on his side, his big brown head lying over the edge of his sofa.

Soon, he had forgotten all about the newspaper and his grandparents and he thought of better things. He thought of walking with his lovely mum and of chasing his tennis ball. He imagined lying on his back with his four legs in the air rolling scratching his back on the nice new white carpet in the lounge. He remembered those great times with his head sticking outside the car window when his lovely mum let him sit on the car seat instead of locked in the back like his grandparents did.

"Why do they lock me up? Can't they understand? I love them," the lonely dog said to himself. He turned his big brown body over to lie curled up in a ball and he sighed. *"Humans, they never learn."*

"That blooming dog!" his grandma shouted to her husband as she brushed Buster's dog hairs off her new sofa and then she grumbled to herself. "Dogs, they never learn."

Buster was a cross bred dog. His parents were a Staffordshire bull terrier and a big brown chocolate Labrador. He had big brown eyes and droopy ears, a long chocolate brown body and legs with a white patch on his big terrier chest. When he grinned, his teeth shone through a wide gaping mouth showing a beautiful Staffordshire terrier smile. He had a long thin round tail which he wagged furiously every time he was happy. Like all Labradors he loved to retrieve his tennis ball and swim in the nearby sea and like all Staffordshire terriers he loved children and he loved to play and talk to them. He didn't talk like a human did but he whined his own language with a familiar Staffordshire sound and accent...something in human sound and speech like.... "oooh, oooh, oooh."

Sadly, his grandparents didn't understand 'Staffy' talk. They thought he was just whining on, making a racket – unnecessarily. However,

Buster also never understood why they never liked his doggy talk. All he was saying was I love you and I always want to be with you. He also never understood that his grandparents did not seem to like him lying on their new furniture. These misunderstandings always led to Buster being locked up in the kitchen. This made him very lonely - but like dogs, and sometimes stubborn people do, he kept doing the same thing and he kept being locked up again.

Then, one fateful day when his grandparents had left him alone, he became very anxious and sad. He really didn't know why he got so upset, and he really didn't want to be sad, but he decided to open the kitchen door and try to find something to cheer him up. He stood on his back legs and turned the door handle with his front paws. Next, he did the same for the lounge door handle. "*Great,*" he thought, "*my new sofa to lie on*" and he climbed onto grandma's new sofa.

After resting a while, he was still sad and lonely so he climbed down and stared at the study door. He'd noticed his grandma had put something from the kitchen in there that morning. "*Maybe its food,*" he wondered, so he opened the door the same way he had the others.

After sniffing around the study for a while, he could smell something through a cupboard door so he opened that and there was the food – two Christmas cakes his grandma had cooked that morning on the cupboard shelf. *"Oh wonderful,"* he thought, *"that will cheer me up"* so he knocked one onto floor, scratched the grease proof paper off and enjoyed chomping on the delicious stuff. But Buster wasn't a greedy dog, just bored, so he played with the cake spreading it across the new study carpet. He soon decided maybe it's time for a sleep, so he left the new fruit and flour toy he'd found and climbed onto the lounge comfy sofa again.

I won't say too much about what happened when Grandma came home and saw her Christmas cake spread over the study and Buster snoring on her posh new sofa. Needless to say, she had a nervous breakdown and the doctor had to be called. Grumpy grandad locked Buster in the kitchen for days as they waited for Buster's mum to visit them from the school where she worked.

Buster's mum was called Miss Wood at school. Her first name was Kitty to her friends and family. She was feeling very sad as she listened to her angry mother complaining over dinner.

"He will have to stay with you at school. We have had enough of his naughtiness. He is always on my lovely sofa and rolling on my new carpet and if I leave the bedroom doors open - on my lovely new duvet. And the doctor has given me more tablets to take for my nerves after the Christmas cake incident. I can't have it Kitty."

"And that blooming whining! He never stops," Kitty's grumpy dad swore. Buster's constant chatting to him drove him even grumpier that he was normally.

"Oh dear," Kitty thought, "here we go again. They really don't understand that Buster only wants to protect them and talk to them. I'll have to do something I think Mum's head might burst and Dad, well, he'll grump himself into hospital."

Her problem was that she worked in a boarding school and because she looked after children who stayed in school at night and weekends until their holidays, she could not keep Buster there. Therefore, her parents had agreed to look after him, but sadly for Kitty, Buster's behaviour was not what her parents expected. She came up with an idea.

"Ok, then parents I'll have to talk to the Headmaster. Maybe he will let him be the classroom dog – a therapy dog for the children. Some schools have a dog in the classroom to help children who have difficulties with other children - the dog helps them socialise with others."

"That big blooming dog won't help the kids. For heaven's sake, he might eat the blooming little horrors!" Kitty's dad swore again. He meant to be joking but it wasn't a very nice thing to say really was it.

Buster who was lying on his own sofa in the kitchen was listening to the conversation and wondered *"why did his grandpa think he would eat children? He loved children. He would only eat anyone who tried to hurt his beloved mother, Kitty or the children. But, if the nice person, the Headmaster, whoever that was, allows him be with his mum all day, well, he'd be a very happy hound."*

He was so happy at the thought that he told them so in his language, wagging his tale furiously in his joy. "Oooh, oooh, oooh," he said out loud.

But his mum's dad misunderstood Buster's chit chat yet again.

"Listen to that the blooming dog. He's whining again and wagging his blooming tail. Why would he do that! Why would he whine miserably and at the same time wag his tail as if he is happy? I tell you the dog's daft. It's time you took him to school Kitty. He's driving us mad."

"You must be mad. I'm trying to tell you I'm happy," Buster said, but no one understood his doggy language. Again, he thought, "*they never learn. I'll get off the sofa and try to show I'm happy. I'll cuddle Grandad and tell him I love him.*"

He slithered off the sofa and came towards the table and went to put his big brown head on his Grandad's lap, hoping to get a nice pat. Instead, he got a huge shock.

"Hzzz, Hzzz, yowl, yowl......!"

A huge hissing and yelling sound arose under the tablecloth and then a loud bang as Buster's big head banged off the wooden table leg. "Woof, woof, grr, grr," he barked out in doggy sounds, as he jumped out from under the table terrified.

"What the heck......!" his Grandad exclaimed terrified and spilling his tea onto his trousers. "What's that blooming dog up to now for heaven's sake? Buster stop that you silly dog."

"It's not Buster dad. It's Izzy, she's sat under the table on the spare chair and scratched him. She always does it. You know that."

"Blooming dog! He's not right in the head," her dad said, knowing fine well that it was the ferocious family ginger and white cat, Izzy, that had lain in wait for the poor dog.

"You know she does it on purpose just to get Buster in trouble," Kitty said. "He's terrified of her. Look, he's shivering, terrified. She's deliberately teasing him now."

Izzy walked slowly past the frightened, shivering dog. His nose was bleeding with a well-aimed claw wound from the crafty feline's ambush under the table. She looked up at him and hissed in cat language.

"Hopefully, that will get you thrown out of MY house at last. You are going to school you stupid canine. Good riddance."

She jumped up past the wounded dog onto the middle of Buster's favourite sofa and sat facing him with her paws under her chest. She pretended to close her eyes, teasing him to dare to climb on.

Buster lay on the hard kitchen floor. His arthritis was hurting but unlike his grumpy grandad, he never whined on about the pain. He was now 13 years old and that was nearly 80 human years in human years. His grey hairs on his muzzle and his aching bones showed his age. He had always been terrified of this hissing spitting evil demon. Even when he was young and fully fit and would fight the fiercest dog or human man who might try to hurt his beloved mum, he was still terrified of Izzy. She was the boss.

She knew this of course - all cats know this. That is why they love to torture dogs and Izzy was delighted she may have finally got rid of this smelly, unclean dog. To emphasise this, she started to nonchalantly lick and clean her paws as she whispered to a very miserable Buster.

"Well, this is my sofa now. Go and stick your head out of the car window when you get taken away like all you stupid canines do. Once you get locked up at school that will be the last fresh air you will smell."

She turned over, rolled and then stretched her ginger body right across Buster's comfy sofa, showing him her brilliant white tummy as if to tempt him to try to chew it. Buster knew from experience he was too slow to try that. She'd have his other nostril with her claws before he got near. He growled quietly using his Grandad's naughty word. "That blooming cat!"

"Listen, he's still growling," Kitty's house-proud mum said, mistaking Buster's frustration at the darned cat for nastiness. "I'm not sure he'll be safe with the kids at school. Our Eva would never growl."

Here we go again Kitty thought *they never understand Buster. Eva can do no wrong. She is lovely but Mum has made her as perfect as her house.*

Eva was a tiny fluffy Miniature Schnauzer. Kitty took a drink of coffee and looked at Eva, lying in her small basket with one eye open and one floppy ear cocked right in the air. She knew Eva was listening to everything. Her dad called her his "German Hound". She was a couple of years older than Buster and they were great friends. Buster protected her from any nasty dog or human but sadly he couldn't protect her from the crazy cat, Izzy.

Poor Eva lay most of the time terrified in her basket as she had lost most of her sight and some of her hearing. Sometimes the cat would stalk the poor sightless hound and then pounce on her grabbing her by her neck and dragging her down like a lion would with an antelope. As Eva picked herself up the cat would stroll off, purring, licking her paws while the small tortured dog shook her curly hair and struggled back to the safety of her basket. Poor Eva often thought the African Savannah with lions prowling was safer than her house.

Buster always growled and barked at Izzy for hunting his friend Eva but the cat always sat looking at Buster, daring him to try his chance with her. She would whisper quietly as she sharpened her claws on Grandma's furniture.

"Do you want a piece of me? Well, just try you stupid hound."

Buster had learned his lesson so he never did dare have a piece of the crazy cat. So, he growled quietly and whined, "oooh, oooh, oooh", trying to tell his owners what had happened. However, as usual he always got the blame for the commotion when his grandparents came running into the room.

Kitty was annoyed that Buster always got the blame. She thought to herself again.

"I got Buster from his rescue home. He had a nasty parent. But Buster is loved and healed now and loves everybody. If only they could see that. It looks like he'll have to come to stay with me at school. I do hope the Headmaster will approve."

The next day she went back to stay at school. Kitty worked in a nearby boarding school. She looked after all the students by day and night from around the world who had come from all over the country and overseas to study. They slept and stayed in the school House each term until the holidays. Buster had to stay with her parents during school times and that was the problem. He missed his mum all the time she was away working. He always slept on her bed and had lain with his mum on her own chairs and sofa at his mum's old home before she had to stay at school with the students. Now he lived with his grandma and she wouldn't let him anywhere near her new furniture.

Back at school Kitty had to face her boss, the Headmaster, Doctor Bruce, and ask if Buster could come to stay. He was quite a stern man with a large, grey haired head. He could sometimes have a loud voice and Kitty was worried he may not understand her need to have Buster with her and that she may have to leave her job she loved. Kitty entered the Doctor Bruce's office hoping that she could make him understand that Buster loved children and nice people.

After listening carefully to Kitty's predicament and patting Buster several times on his big brown head, the Headmaster sat back in his chair and thought for a while. Then to her joy and delight the Headmaster agreed that Buster was a lovely friend and companion and he could come to school.

"But you must keep him in your apartment Miss Wood until we are sure he is alright with children in the classroom," the great man explained.

Kitty was delighted and so was Buster when he found out. Wagging his tail happily he whined a thank you to his mum, "oooh, oooh, oooh..."

Buster was going to school.

CHAPTER TWO
BUSTER DROWNS THE HEADMASTER

Doctor Bruce had said that Buster must settle in first and show his best behaviour before he would allow him to be a classroom dog and Buster did just that.

He was so happy at school and loved walking in the grounds and playing with the students in the boarding house at night. He soon became friends with the Junior School students his mum looked after. They came to talk to him through the door every day while they went to their lessons. Every night he would play with them in the common room and during his own walks and playtime.

Buster soon came to settle down while he was locked in his mum's apartment and looked forward every day to when he could hear the children outside his door coming and going to their dormitory and common room. He always talked to them through the door:

"Oooh, oooh, oooh," he shouted through the gap under the floor. And the children chatted back to him in kind human language.

After a few weeks at school Buster was so happy that he decided that the next time he saw the Headmaster he would say thank you for being so nice to his mum and him. The very next day he got the chance. Kitty had taken Buster for his usual walk around the beautiful school grounds on her lunch break. He ran and ran after his tennis ball as his mum threw it with the long plastic dog ball thrower. He retrieved it and dropped it back at his mum' feet every time, eagerly wagging his tail and watching the ball intently, waiting for her to throw it again and again. Then, Buster saw the Headmaster taking a lunchtime stroll through the gardens. Buster was delighted and excited.

"I must thank him for being so kind to mum," Buster said. "I'll take him my ball to throw."

Doctor Bruce had experienced a very difficult morning on the telephone. He had spoken to several people about the new pupil who was coming to the school. He was both excited and worried about the student's arrival. The school which was 200 years old and situated on a beautiful part of England's coast line had taken quite a few famous people over its history but never one as famous as now. Many parents from overseas sent their children but never had a parent so famous as this wish their child to be placed in his hands – Doctor Bruce had not expected that phone call and he had a lot on his mind as he took his usual lunchtime exercise stroll around the school grounds. He didn't expect Buster either.

Buster ran excitedly to the Head of School and stopped as he reached him. He dropped his green tennis ball at the startled gentleman's feet.

"Buster! What are you doing here? You should be in your apartment," the man said, mildly annoyed his peace had been disturbed. He clumsily kicked Buster's ball away and he carried on walking.

Buster was overjoyed. The man wanted to play!

So, he ran and retrieved the ball and dropped the soggy tennis ball in front of the esteemed Principal of the School's feet again. This time the Headmaster didn't kick the ball away. He shook his head at Buster and he kept on walking. Buster realised that Doctor Bruce did not want to play.

"If the man won't kick or throw my ball maybe this is the time to give him a thank you for letting me stay with mum" the happy dog thought. So, Buster took two steps and he jumped up, putting his two paws onto the Headmaster's shoulders. Then, much to the great man's horror, the big brown beast gave him a great big slurpy kiss.

Unfortunately, this so shocked Doctor Bruce that he wobbled and toppled backwards into the pond.

Kitty looked at the drowned man horrified as some teachers and pupils came running over to help. Buster sat down, cocked his head and looked at his mum and then moved his head to the drowning man and back to his mum again. He didn't understand what the fuss was about.

"I thought humans like to swim?" he said in his own whining language. However, it came out to the human folks around as, "oooh, ooh, oooh."

"What's that blooming dog whining on for! It's me who should be angry. Get me out of here!" Doctor Bruce shouted to his deputy head. His deputy took his leader's hand and she pulled him out of the pond.

The Headmaster emerged dripping wet with pond weed in his hair, pulling small frogs and tadpoles from his jacket pockets. Everyone wanted to laugh but wisely they kept silent until they knew how the fierce man would react. Buster, looking around and seeing no smiles or hearing any laughter, felt a little guilty, so he thought he'd better apologise.

"Oooh, oooh, oooh," he said in his 'Staffy' language, meaning, "I'm very, very sorry. Please don't be cross."

"Miss Wood!" the bedraggled Headmaster shouted at Kitty. "I thought I told you to keep that animal in the apartment when school was in session. And stop him whining. What on earth is wrong with him? It's me who is soaked."

Doctor Bruce wiped the mud and frogs off his gown, threw the pond weed back into the pond and stormed off. The students who saw the incident chuckled at it all and immediately started posting pictures of their bedraggled, soaked Headmaster on their social media. A very wet Dr Bruce received over 10,000 likes on Instagram that afternoon alone. He was becoming famous - all because of Buster.

Kitty kneeled down, picked up all the tiny amphibian beasts and placed them back in the pond. Buster was nudging her, trying to say sorry, but she pushed him away and scolded him.

"I really didn't need that Buster. Why can't you behave like a normal dog? I'll now have to leave you longer each day. You are not going to like that are you?"

Buster didn't like the idea he would not get a walk at break time but he thought *"at least I'm with my mum and can sleep in her bed and lie on her sofa. Maybe it won't be that bad."*

At the same time the Headmaster was also thinking. However, he wasn't thinking of playing with tennis balls, comfy sofa's and beds. He was thinking:

"How on earth are we going to cope with the President of the United States' ten-year-old son attending my School?"

What he didn't know was that there were some very dangerous and bad people who were also thinking what they were going to do with his new famous schoolboy.

CHAPTER THREE
BUSTER GOES TO THE VET

After drowning the Headmaster poor Buster was locked up in his mum's apartment all day after his long morning walk before school. He had to wait now until she could get a break and walk with him again.

After an initial sadness he settled down very well but was bored. He spent his days lying on the small sofa thinking of walking in the woods, swimming in the lovely sea and digging huge holes in the sand on the beautiful beaches surrounding his home. Most of all he dreamed of retrieving his tennis ball from the sea or the wide expanses of the high moors on which he loved to roam. When he dreamed he made a different sound to that which he talked to his family and friends. It was but more of a soft, "woof, woof, growl, and woof". If he got excited in his dream, he would shout out in his whining language, "oooh, oooh, oooh."

The children as they returned from day school to their dormitory to collect books heard Buster dreaming and they whispered nice words through the door to him to help him sleep. But one day Buster's life and nice doggy dreams changed to nightmares when a new boy arrived at the school.

He came the same day the very important American President's son arrived. He was from London and seemed very unhappy to be there. He first met Buster after school when his mum brought Buster on his leash to see the students in their common room.

"Hello, you are new, aren't you? Bradley isn't it? I'm Miss Wood your boarding teacher and this is Buster the school dog," she said to the boy, standing sulking with his hands in his pockets.

"Is he a pet?" the new boy said.

"Yes. He's a friend to everyone who stays here. He wants to be your friend too while you stay here, Bradley," said Miss Wood. "Do you have a pet at home?"

Bradley looked up at his boarding mistress, shrugged his shoulders and spoke. "No. Dad hates pets. He says dogs should be used to fight or to run for money. We've never had a pet and I don't want one now."

And he walked away, pushing a smaller boy on the arm and saying. "Who are you staring at?" as he swaggered off to his bedroom staring menacingly at his fellow students.

Bradley was a London boy, 10 years old and a big boy for his age. He spoke with a broad London accent. He had blonde hair which was very untidy and reached his shoulders. His new black blazer was tight on his large shoulders and his grey trousers were baggy on his stocky legs. His new black shoes were already scuffed and dirty. His face was long and hard and his nose had been squashed in some way. He looked a very tough boy and his manner with his fellow boarders showed that. However, Miss Wood noticed in his big brown eyes a hint of sadness and possibly fear but until she got to know him she couldn't tell which.

Kitty took Buster to the other students to play. She was still thinking a lot about Bradley. *"Maybe he is scared and lonely his first day on his own I'll try to make him feel safe and at home here. Everyone feels lonely at first but we all get on with each other in the end and enjoy it. I'm sure this boy will come around."*

Bradley sat on his bed. He took off his blazer and flung it across the room with his tie. He kicked off his shoes and fell back onto the bed staring at the ceiling. He was still angry. He didn't want to be here, all these miles away from his friends and his family. He had been happy at his old school. His dad had told him he had to go away because he wanted him to spy on the American President's son who was at the school here and report back everything about the school and what the boy did.

He knew his dad was an angry and important man who was boss of a gang of many other dangerous large men. He didn't know what things they got up to but he didn't think they were very nice. The police had been to Bradley's large mansion of a house several times to talk with his father but had never seemed to have arrested him.

"*He must know what he is doing I guess,*" Bradley often thought. "*But this! Spying on someone so important. How dangerous was that!*" Bradley thought. "*If he's the President's son there will be armed Secret Service people guarding him. They might shoot me !*"

He tried to tell his father that he wouldn't go to the school because it was too dangerous but his father wouldn't listen. And when Bradley insisted he wasn't going, his father hit him. Bradley was hurt and scared so he agreed he would do what his violent father asked. And now he was here and he had already upset his fellow school friends.

He sat up on his bed and winced in pain, remembering his father's blows. He felt the bruises which his father had given him which still hurt on his back. "*Yes, his father could be an angry man,*" he thought, "*I had better do what he wants this time.*"

He stood up and pulled on his sweat shirt, put on some jeans and trainers and went back to the common room to make friends with the

President of the United States' son as his father had instructed him to do.

The next morning Bradley was walking past Miss Wood's apartment door and he saw a couple of girls at the door laughing and talking to the door. "What are you soft idiots doing? All girls are crazy to me," he said nastily.

"We're not crazy. All boys are stupid to me," said Zahra and she tried to push past Bradley but he pushed her against the corridor wall.

"We were only cheering Buster up. He's having a nightmare. We talk to him every day," shouted Emily as she ran across the room. "Leave her alone," she shouted as she grabbed Zahra and they walked away. As they reached the boarding house door to the main school, they both shouted back. "Buster is our friend. You are just a bully."

Bradley stood and grunted. "A bully eh, and that stupid dog is their friend. Daft girls, I'll show them." And he banged violently on Miss Wood's door.

Buster was dreaming again of happy days chasing his ball. He had listened half asleep to his friends Zahra and Emily talking to him with nice words and felt very happy at the sound of their calming voices. Then he was shaken awake by the loud banging on his mums' door.

"What on earth!" he shouted out in his language. Then he panicked, "someone is trying to break in and hurt the children or, dear me, maybe my mum." He jumped off his sofa and ran to the door barking loudly. "Woof! Woof! Woof!"

Bradley laughed and started kicking the door. He shouted out in a nasty loud voice. "Come on you daft dog. Where's your friends now eh!"

Buster barked louder and climbed up at the door, scratching and whining. "Oooh, oooh, oooh."

Bradley bent down and spoke to Buster horridly under the door. "You stupid dog!" and he growled under the door, "grrr, grrr, ggrr."

"Oooh, oooh , oooh," Buster shouted out and then barked loudly.

"Just like dad says," Bradley said to himself, "dogs are stupid. They should be whipped and kept to fight or make money. They are not friends." And he kicked the door and bent down and shouted "Grrr, grrr, grrr," through the bottom of the door again and again.

He laughed and laughed as he listened to Buster barking and whining. Pleased with his torturing Buster he turned, walked a few paces and opened the boarding house door to school.

"Stupid dog. I hope they take him to the dog pound," he laughed as he slammed shut the door.

Poor Buster was tormented as he lay on his sofa. He kept whining saying out loud to anyone who would listen, "Why would anyone be so horrid and bang and grrr at my mum's door?"

Buster managed to get back to sleep after a few hours of feeling very worried, panting and pacing up and down in the room. He started dreaming again, when suddenly, there was a huge banging on his door and a familiar voice was shouting through the gap under the door.

"Heh! You stupid dog. Wake up! It's me Bradley again." And still banging on the door he growled at the dog, "grrr , grrr , grrr , grrr."

Buster ran over to the door barking and whining and the whole horrible episode for him was repeated. Buster was whining and pleading for someone to come and stop it all.

No one could understand Buster that night when he tried to tell Mum and her friends as they walked with him about what had happened to him with Bradley.

"What's wrong with Buster tonight Kitty?" Frau Weizmann, the German teacher asked.

"He's certainly upset about something. Aren't you Buster?" said Mrs Roberts the Head of Boarding School, patting the sad hound on his proud brown head.

"Oooh, oooh, oooh," Buster whined to them, meaning - "That new boy, he's not happy. He needs help."

"I think Buster's just missing people during the day," answered Kitty. "Why he's started now I have no idea."

And horribly for his mum, and for Buster, Bradley carried on tormenting Buster every day that first week he was at school.

Finally, Buster could take no more and he cracked. He began whining all day and he showed again what a magician he was with door handles and opened his locked kitchen window to bark for attention. Sadly, he climbed half way out and jammed his body in the frame. Frightened and scared, he whined and barked. All the students and staff were distressed at poor Buster's plight and sent a student to bring his mum.

31

Then the Headmaster came running to see what the fuss was. He was cross at the disturbance to his quiet school. Buster's mum arrived in tears very upset at the poor animal's plight and she ran up to her room to rescue and comfort him.

After this incident Doctor Bruce asked Kitty to come and see him. He told a distraught Miss Wood she must do something about her dog and keep him locked up and keep him silent. Poor Buster everyone in the school, except Bradley, thought.

Buster's mum Kitty was so worried why his behaviour had changed that she decided to take him to the Emergency Vet. The veterinary surgeon was a lovely lady who knew Buster and he was so gentle with her. She examined him with her stethoscope and took his blood through a large syringe and needle. She listened carefully to his mum tell her of Buster's problems and finally the Vet told her what was wrong.

"It seems Buster has what we call anxiety. Some humans and dogs get the same thing when they have worries and problems in their heads. Dogs are prone to a thing called separation anxiety which means they get really depressed and also anxious if they are not with their loved ones. They can destroy furniture, wail, bark and try to get to people they love anyway they can. I am sure that is Buster's problem."

"Oh dear, poor Buster," Kitty sighed, almost in tears. "What can I do? I can't be with him all day. I have to work and he can't be on his own out of his room at school."

"Well, I can give him some tablets that will calm him down. They are called Prozac. People use them to cheer them up when they are depressed and have anxiety. Sometimes they work very well with dogs."

"Will they make him sleepy? I really don't want him doped up on drugs," Kitty asked.

"Not particularly but just calmer. What you can also do is play nice music to him or put the radio on all day. That helps them think someone is with them and it calms them. Try that and let me know how it all goes."

So, Buster ended up taking what once was the world's best-selling medicine for anxiety in humans and his mum bought him his own radio to listen to everyday. He certainly was a unique dog.

But his problems with Bradley were about to start all over again.

CHAPTER FOUR
BUSTER MEETS A NEW FRIEND

Bradley laughed when he heard in the common room that Buster had been taken to the emergency Vet and that he now was on tablets and listened to pop music.

"The dog's stupid. All dogs are. You must all be stupid too, talking to him like you do. He must be psycho if he's been treated by the head doctor. One day he'll eat you all," he blurted out to the students who were talking with the new boy from America about Buster.

"I hope he eats you," shouted Emily to the nasty laughing boy and turning to her friend she said. "What do you think Zahra?"

Zahra was Emily's friend and she had been a refugee from another country and had come to the country a few years ago with her mother and brother. She had been very lonely at first but she adapted well and when her parents were reunited after the war they came to live near the school. She was a very positive young lady and having been through so much hatred and hurt she liked everyone to get on with each other. She disliked bullies and people who called others names because they were from a different country, race or colour and she was not scared of telling them they were wrong.

Zahra walked over to where Bradley was sat on his own reading his smart phone and stood in front of him. She scowled at him and spoke. "I'm not scared of you. Buster's only started getting poorly since you came. It wouldn't surprise me if you are the cause. I think you are sick. Maybe Miss Wood should take you to the vet."

"Let them try. My father is a very rich. He is a tough and important man in London. He has many men working for him. He'd sort out anyone here who tried to hurt me."

"By the looks of the bruises on your body I saw in the showers the other day, I'd say he is quite happy to hurt his own kids," interrupted the American President's son, who had finally begun to settle in with his fellow boarders.

"Don't you say that, I'll, I'll .... thump you.... you, you ...," stuttered an angry Bradley, stopping his sentence before saying the nasty word that he really wanted to say about the President's son.

"You, you.... what? What did you mean to call me?" said the President's son very calmly, standing up and facing Bradley. Some of the other boarders also stood up to support him.

Bradley looked around and knew he was outnumbered. He was a bully but clever. He'd get his own back in his own time. He started walking to the door and looked at them all and muttered with his head bowed.

"I can say what I like. You'll never stop me. I'm not scared of any of you. You don't like me and I don't care. If I tell my dad, watch what he does to your precious school and that stupid dog." And he slammed the door shut and went to his bedroom.

"Good riddance to him," Zahra said, and she introduced the new boy to a big brown, tail wagging hound.

"Buster this is Leon. Leon this is Buster."

Leon scratched the happy dog's neck and patted his sides firmly. "What a beautiful dog you are Buster. Don't worry about that Bradley dude. You and me are buddies now. I'll see he doesn't bother you." And turning to his new friends he said. "That Bradley boy has some issues for sure. I think he needs some help folks, maybe we should try to help him come clean about what's bugging him?"

Emily frowned, took the President's son's arm and remarked. "Forget him Leon. He is just nasty and bad. His father must beat him a lot to make him like that. I think he'll soon be found out and kicked out. Doctor Bruce is a clever man and Miss Wood is so kind, they will see through his wickedness and kick him out."

"Nope, I think I'll make it my mission to help the dude. My mom always says everyone needs a

break sometimes girl," said Leon smiling. And he
rubbed Buster's ears saying, "Come on boy let's
see if you like to dance. Do you like Hip Hop my
canine buddy?"

He switched his cell phone to play music from
the Wi Fi. He played a couple of tracks of Drake
and Kendrick Lamar and he began to dance in
the common room.

Buster cocked his head to one side and
watched his new friend dancing. He cocked it
the other way to watch Zahra take Leon's hand
and dance as well. "*That's nice music,*" he
thought and he began to feel much happier.

"Maybe Buster would like to hear something
that reminds him of his mum's voice - a lady
singing perhaps? Have you any Leon?" asked
Emily, as she stroked Buster's head.

"Yeah, I've got lots. Maybe he'll like this," and
he switched tracks on his phone.

"Yes, that's better I think, look at Buster's
face and tail," said Emily, "he really likes me and
the music. Come on Buster let's dance!"

Buster was so happy that he began to sing
himself, "ooh, ooh, ooh." And as he whined, he
circled around the three dancing kids with a
huge smile on his face.

Miss Wood came into the room delighted at the sight of her happy students and her happy dog. "Wow, that's good dancing Leon and I like the song. Who is it?"

"Do you wanna dance Miss?" Leon said, slowing the tempo down of his dance.

"No thank you Leon. It's time you lot were in your rooms. But if you'd show me the link to that music I'd like to listen to it as well. And maybe, this will be the music that helps Buster with his separation anxiety." She looked at a very happy Buster who was curling up on an old worn-out sofa, "I have a feeling that Buster would love that too."

"Heh, sure Miss. I've an old smart phone and speakers and I'll program a shed load of her music for the dude and give it to you. I'll even play it for him from my phone through his door everyday when I go between lessons and chit chat with him. Maybe we'll get him dancing as well. What do you think buddy," Leon said, breaking into a huge laugh as he picked up Buster's two front legs and danced with him around the common room.

All the students began laughing and Buster, thinking they were happy, began laughing his own way as he danced by whining in unison: "Ooo, oooh, ooo!"

Miss Wood laughed along with all the students as Leon and Buster danced. She was so happy that Buster was now feeling much better, hopefully soon he would be cured of his separation anxiety and Doctor Bruce would let him become a classroom dog.

But she didn't know what horrible things Bradley and his father were planning and what was going to happen to poor Buster.

CHAPTER FIVE
BUSTER IS BULLIED AGAIN

Bradley never forgot his humiliation by Leon and he blamed Buster.

"I'll get my own back on that dog and that Yank. Just wait till my dad and his gang come here to kidnap the smug Yank. That'll make the girls who think he's lovely cry," he uttered to himself lying on his bed, grinning widely.

For terribly, that was the reason his father had placed him in the school, to spy on Leon and the school security. His father was a very dangerous man who led a notorious gang of criminals in London. He intended to kidnap the President's son and ransom him for millions of American dollars but he needed his son's help to do that. Bradley smiled nastily when he thought how his father may hurt Leon if he didn't co-operate. But he stopped smiling and grimaced when he remembered how much his violent father had beaten him when he said he didn't want to do this terrible thing. And the big tough bully Bradley began to cry.

Meanwhile, every day after the argument with Bradley, Leon walked past Buster in his mum's room and chuckled when he heard the hushed sounds of the music of Leon's favourite hip hop singers coming through the door. He always spoke softly through the door to Buster who then leapt from his bed on his mum's sofa to sing and dance with him through the door.

"Oooh, oooh, ooh," Buster whined standing on his back legs with his front feet against the door as if he was singing and dancing to the music and Leon's voice.

At break times Leon would come upstairs to the boarding dormitory and play new songs through the door to Buster. Buster liked this music and he started to become much happier in his lonely separation anxiety. That was until Bradley spoiled it all....

Bradley hated to hear the students talking in the common room after school about how Leon had cured Buster. The bully sulked and whispered nasty things to other boarders when Leon and Buster danced together with Zahra and Emily in common room after school. Leon tried to teach them all his hip hop dance moves to music from his favourite bands J-Z, Eminem and others, and Buster danced but he really liked the R n B music of Beyoncé, Adele and other singers his mum liked.

Bradley was so jealous of Leon's popularity with his fellow schoolmates that he began saying horrible things them and spreading untrue nasty messages on social media about Leon. But most of all he hated Buster for making Leon so popular. So, he made a plan to cause the poor dog trouble.

Every day when Buster was listening to his lovely music in his mum's room when no one was looking Bradley banged on the door again. He shouted horrible things at Buster. He rattled the door handle and pushed his ruler under the door teasing the dog even more. Buster sadly got very cross and confused. Eventually, he scratched and howled at the door barking loudly and instead of singing to the music he started whining loudly in a hurt and angry way. "Oooh, oooh, oooh, woof, woof."

Friendly teachers and students asked Kitty to come upstairs from her lessons each day to calm Buster down. She had to take more time to walk him around the lovely grounds of the school. However, eventually Mr Bruce heard about Buster's disturbance of his nice orderly school timetable and the noise disturbing his perfect classrooms.

"If he doesn't improve Miss Wood, I'm afraid you'll have to take him back to his grandparents," he told his distressed teacher. "Can the vet not give him some more medicine?"

"I don't know Doctor Bruce," Kitty replied holding back her tears. "I really don't know why he has gone back to his ways. He loves Leon and his music and he was much better and happy. Something has changed. Maybe the Vet can help. I'll go tonight."

So, Buster went off to the vet yet again.

"I think we will increase the dose of Prozac. It will act more of a sedative and he'll sleep more. But if that doesn't work we will have to give him a real sedative," the vet advised.

"I don't want him sleepy all day, it's not fair. He loves his music and Leon. If the Prozac doesn't work, I'll have no choice but to take him to my parents' house and I don't think that will work for Buster or them. He really loves the children at school . I really am so upset," Kitty told the vet and then her tears fell down her face.

Buster was distressed to see and hear his owner and mum cry. He nuzzled his nose onto her legs and began to whine. "Ooh, ooh, ooo," meaning, "don't cry Mum. It's that horrible boy Bradley. It's not me."

Kitty smiled and patted his head gently, not understanding his words but knowing he was trying to comfort her. "I know Buster, I know. You are a good boy. We'll work this out."

And she said thank you to the Vet and put Buster into the back of her car and drove back to school.

Buster lay in the car thinking. *"Oh dear, I love my grandparents and Eva but that psychotic cat Izzy scares me too much. I think she will eat me* one day if I sleep too much. And Grandad will bash me with his paper and Grandma will have a nervous breakdown again if I lie on her settee....oh dear, I must try to ignore that nasty boy's teasing for my lovely mum's sake."

And he closed his eyes and dreamed of dancing with Beyoncé.

But very soon something horrible would happen that would soon turn his happy sleep into a dangerous nightmare.

CHAPTER SIX
BUSTER HEARS A TERRIBLE THING

The next day Leon was very kind to Buster and he played the latest Beyoncé hit *'Crazy in Love'* through the door. He spoke gently to Buster hoping to ease his worries. "Don't worry dude we'll get you through this. I wish you could tell me what's bugging you. You are fine until I leave you. What is upsetting you during the day buddy?"

Buster whined. "Ooh ooh ooh." Meaning- "It's that boy Bradley, he teases me every day."

Of course, Leon didn't understand dog talk and he replied. "I know Buster, you miss your mum and so do I miss mine. She is so far away and always busy with running the country. I'm lonely too. I'll try to help you buddy, as your friend. Give me a high five dude." And he placed a high five hand on the door. Buster placed his two front feet on the other side at the same time, giving a high ten with his paws.

Meanwhile, Bradley had more pressing things to worry about than teasing Buster. His angry father had told him down his smart phone the night before. "Next week it's their Speech Day. It will get busy there soon so we have to come down tomorrow night. We need you to open the back door into the school and show us the way. You must block out the lens of the security camera with sticky tape and you put the sleeping pills I sent you into Leon's bodyguard's coffee. Can you do that son?"

"I can't climb that high to fix the cameras and there are two of them. And how am I going to put pills in the Secret Service man's drink? He doesn't come near us; he sleeps in a room next to

Miss Wood. They always have a cup of coffee in their kitchen. I can't do it Dad, I'm scared," Bradley blurted out, almost shaking with worry.

His father screamed down the phone at his frightened son. "You will do it or you'll get my belt on your backside again. Dope that silly teacher up as well; give her a double dose with the Secret Service man. We can't risk her waking up. If it kills them well so be it, we will be millionaires when we get that American brat ransomed and you can leave that backwoods town and come back to the big city with me."

Bradley held his phone trembling with fear and realised that he really didn't want to go back to his violent dad or the big city. He was starting to like being free of his bullying father and the violence he lived with inside the city. Here in the country, it was fresh air, rolling hills and clear sea and even palm trees, and he was finally starting to like his fellow kids. But he was scared of another beating and he really would like to get his own back on that smug Yank and that blooming dog. So, he bit his tongue and held back his tears and told his father he'd have everything done that he asked.

"We will be outside that back door at exactly one a.m. tomorrow night. Make sure the alarm and camera are off and that that Secret Service man is well doped up. If you mess this up, don't bother coming back home," his nasty father growled and abruptly ended the call.

Bradley lay on his bed wondering how he was going to do what his father wanted. What he didn't know was that Buster had been listening to his call. Dogs have hearing almost as acute as their sense of smell, much better than humans and he had wandered down the boarding corridor when he heard the loud voice of Bradley's screaming father through the telephone. He got there just in time to hear the human words: "dope that silly teacher up" and "it doesn't matter if it kills them". He panicked and began whining for help and scratching at Bradley's bedroom door.

"Oooh oooh!, woof woof." Which meant - "Help? Help! He's going to hurt my mum."

Leon and the other kids came running and Leon shouted as he grabbed Buster's big leather collar. "What's up Buster! Has he been teasing you buddy?' and he pulled Buster away from the door and banged on the bedroom door shouting.

"Come out you coward! See if you can bully someone your size."

But Bradley stayed behind his door. He wasn't going to risk a fight with Leon. He shouted through the door. "I've done nothing. It's that dog, he's a mental case. He's even on drugs. Go away or I'll call 999 and get the police to shoot it."

"Come on Leon, he's evil enough to do that," Zahra said. She took Buster by his collar and led him back to Miss Wood, who was sitting drinking coffee in the kitchen with the Secret Service Man.

"What's up Buster," said the Secret Service man, rubbing the dog's head and ears. He liked Buster and Buster liked him. "Are there bad guys out there?" he said jokingly.

Buster cocked his head to the guard and whined. "Ooh, ooh." Meaning – "of course there are baddies, they are coming tomorrow. Please protect my mum."

"Something has spooked your dog, Kitty. They see ghosts you know. Maybe the school has a ghost? He said laughing at the thought.

"Come on Buster. It's time for your bed. Zahra thanks for bringing him. It's time for your bed too. Let's get the house boarded down," Miss Wood said, getting up and locking Buster in her room before making sure all the students were in their bedrooms.

Buster laid awake thinking. He was never going to sleep tonight. He knew that.

'What on earth could he do to stop the bad people taking Leon and hurting his mum and her friend?"

CHAPTER SEVEN
BUSTER MEETS THE BADDIES

That day two people could not focus on what they should be focussing on. Bradley couldn't listen in class and was given extra preparation work to do after school and Buster couldn't listen to his music. Both were worried about what might happen that evening.

Bradley realised he would need a ladder to get up to the security cameras so he sneaked out at lunchtime and stole Tommy the maintenance man's ladder. He hid it under the hedge which faced the back door. He left the sticky tape and a sharp knife with it. He also sneaked back to the boarding house to put the powdered sleeping tablets into the milk that Miss Wood used to make the night time coffee. As he left, he banged on her door shouting at Buster one last time he hoped.

"I'll put the rest of the tablets into your biscuit bowl, once we've sorted that Yank friend of yours out. That'll get rid of you forever, you stupid mental dog."

Buster barked and barked at his tormentor but no one came to help. Finally, exhausted with barking, he laid down on his settee and thought of a plan to save his mum and Leon.

That evening Kitty walked Buster as she did every evening. She threw his tennis ball for him across the extensive school fields and he brought it back with his tail wagging fiercely. But he was only pretending because he was about to put his careful plan into action. Kitty fired the ball thrower down towards gates. Buster ran, picked up the ball and ran right outside of the school gates.

Buster! Buster! Come back!" Kitty shouted, terrified he might get run over by a car. He had never done that, ever. She shouted and shouted running to find her beloved friend. She called time and again. "Come back Buster, please!"

Buster was so upset to hear the pain in his mum's voice. When he heard her voice break, he nearly ran back, but he knew had to be strong for his plan to work. Only he could save his beloved mum and his friend Leon.

He had a cunning canine plan....

The teachers and boarders had searched up and down the roads looking for Buster most of the evening. Now they had settled down back at school.

"Don't worry Miss Wood," the Headmaster said. And he asked, "Maybe he ran home to your parents?"

"No, they haven't seen him," Kitty said, her eyes red with crying. "I've asked all the vets to look out for him and phoned the police. I'm so worried. He's never done this before."

"I'm sure he'll turn up," said Doctor Bruce. "I want you to go to bed and rest. I'll take over your duties this evening."

Buster lay wide awake safe only a hundred metres away. He had run up the pavement next to school walls and sneaked into a large garden of an empty house that bordered the school and hid in an old garden shed. He lay there while they searched for him. When night fell his plan was to sneak back in under the garden fence to the school. As Bradley came with his ladder he would run out and bark and bark and bring the teachers and security to catch him and the bad guys. He hoped his mum was not so upset about him running away but he had to do it - he could never let them hurt her.

Meanwhile, back in school the students were safely boarded down and Doctor Bruce and the Secret Service man sat down to share a cup of coffee. Kitty couldn't sleep so she joined them chatting. However, soon they were all fast asleep at the table – drugged by Bradley's sleeping pills.

Bradley looked at his watch. It was 12.30 am. He sneaked out of his bedroom and went into the kitchen where the three sleeping people were. He looked in Miss Wood's pockets for her Boarding House keys. She didn't have them! Shocked he began to tremble, thinking, *"where on earth are the keys to boarding house door?"* Then he remembered Doctor Bruce had locked them all up that evening, so shaking with nerves he looked in the fearsome man's pockets.

"Magic," he whispered as he found them. He

crept out and opened the boarding house door and hurried down the stairs.

Next, he opened the door to the school courtyard and went to the hedge to get his ladder. He placed the ladder against the wall where the camera was, took his tape and knife and began to climb up. Once he was at the top of the ladder he could see his father and two men waiting behind the back door in the back street. He had the code to open the door but he wouldn't do that until the security camera that pointed to the door was covered with his tape.

His father spoke angrily in a loud whisper. "Hurry up you stupid kid. Get a move on. Mess this up and I'll thump you."

Bradley was terrified of his father and he trembled as he cut the tape and stuck it over the camera. He dropped the knife and tape with a small bang as they rattled the ladder.

"You idiot kid, stop that noise. You'll bring the whole blooming police force on us. Open this blooming door!" his father swore at him.

Bradley put the four-number code into the lock and opened the large barred gate. His father slapped him around the head. "Get back up that ladder and tape that other camera pointing to the school."

Bradley climbed the ladder, his head hurt a lot from his father's blow but it seemed to have made him realise that his father was not a nice man. He could see clearly now that this was a very bad thing that he was doing but he was still too scared of his father to stop. He reached the top. Then, trembling as he cut the tape and placed it over the camera, he stumbled, slipped and fell tumbling down from the top.

He landed heavily next to the bad guys. His father kicked him. "You stupid idiot, get up, we can't wait for clumsy fools like you."

But Bradley couldn't get up. He had fallen on the knife and it was stuck through his leg. He was bleeding massively and he couldn't move. "I'm hurt. I'm hurt!" he sobbed.

His father shrugged his shoulders and said to his two thugs. "We'll leave him. He's too much trouble now." And looking down at his wounded son he told him a very hurtful thing. "You'll be alright. It's only a scratch. Tell the police you heard something outside and went to see why the boarding room door was open and the bad guys caught you with their knife." And he crept lower and menacingly whispered. "Keep your mouth shut about anything else. Or else ...."

And the kidnappers hurried towards the open boarding House door.

Buster woke with a start. He was sure he wouldn't sleep but he must have dosed off. He shook himself as he stood up. He looked into sky and saw that the moon was well risen, its moonlight glistening over the shining sea. "*Oh dear*," he said to himself, realising that he'd overslept. He shook himself vigorously and then without a moment lost he rushed towards the boarding house.

Bradley was weeping as his blood leaked over the courtyard. He was in intense pain. "Why did he leave me?" he cried. He was becoming unconscious with the loss of blood. Then he felt a warm wet feeling on his face. He opened his eyes to see Buster's face staring over him, licking his face to wake and comfort him. He cried out weakly, terrified of the dog he'd been bullying. "No! Not you. Please don't bite me. I'm sorry what I did to you. Please don't hurt me. I'm so sorry."

But Buster was gentle and licked him, talking in dog language. "Oooh, oooh, ooh. I won't hurt you if you are sorry. I only want to like you."

Buster was worried. *'What should he do? This poor boy needs a doctor and my mum and Leon are in danger. I can't help everyone."*

Then, he remembered Mrs Roberts the Head of Boarding lived in the cottage in the grounds. *"I must help Bradley first"* he thought, *"he's dying."* He gave Bradley one more lick to comfort him and he ran with all his speed to the cottage, barking as loud as he could.

Mrs Roberts woke up; her older son was staying with her and he woke up too. They both looked out of the window and saw Buster barking like anything at the house.

"It's Buster. He's back. Kitty will be pleased. Go and get him George," the teacher said.

George tried to catch Buster but he kept turning back towards the boarding House and running back to him barking. "There's something up mum. Buster is trying to get me to go to the school. I'm running off with him. I think you should phone the police. I'm worried there is something very bad that's happened."

And George ran with Buster towards the school.

"Oh my God," George said when he saw Bradley and all the blood. "What on earth has happened here?"

He opened his mobile and phoned 999. "I need an ambulance quick please," he said, and then seeing the knife, he added, "and bring the police, I think there has been an attack on a school boy."

Buster couldn't wait for the ambulance as his beloved Mum was in danger. He turned and ran with all his strength through the boarding house door and up the stairs. He ran through into the boarding corridor just in time to see the three men pulling a struggling Leon from his room. His mouth had been taped up and his hands tied. Leon looked pleadingly at Buster. Buster saw the fear in Leon's eyes and he got angry for the first time. He growled and barked and threw himself at the men, baring his ferocious fangs and biting them on their legs and arms. They dropped Leon and tried to punch and kick Buster but he did not feel the blows he was too angry and wanted to protect his friend.

Doors opened and the other boarders saw the commotion, a few ran back into their room and phoned the police, some came to help Buster. When they saw they were outnumbered, the kidnappers ran with Buster chasing them down the stairs, biting the bottom of the ugliest one who screamed out holding his backside. "Blooming dog! Oooh my bum, my bum!"

They ran right into the courtyard just as the police arrived. George rugby tackled one as he tried to run past him. A policeman tasered another one who came at him with a knife he'd pulled from his jacket. Buster watched puzzled as the man's hair spiked and sparkled an electric blue colour like the mad professor on his mum's television he'd once seen. "*Humans are strange,*" he thought.

Then, he saw Bradley's father escape. The coward had left his men to face the police and had sneaked around the side of the courtyard and was now running in the darkness. But Buster could see in the dark much better than humans and he ran after the awful man.

The leader of the gang of kidnappers thought he'd escaped the police and he stopped. He leant against a tree, his chest heaving out of breath, whispering to himself with a big grin on his face. Well, at least I got away safely. My boy and the men will never talk to police. Too scared of what I'll do to all of them."

Then a big brown shape with huge white teeth leapt out of the darkness hit him solidly in his chest.

"What on Earth!" he howled. He staggered backwards a short way, wobbled to and fro twice and fell backwards - straight into the school pond.

Bradley's dad lay almost drowned in the murky water covered in water lilies. He was coughing and spluttering pond water and small tadpoles out of his mouth. He looked up to see what the big thunderbolt was that hit him and he stared into the big brown eyes and open panting mouth of his own nightmare.

Buster stood guard over him. He cocked his head curiously, trying to remember where he had last seen a human drowning in this pond but he couldn't seem to recall. But quickly he remembered why he'd deliberately pushed this horrible human into the pond and knew he had to warn the helpful humans. He began barking as loudly as he could, baring his teeth through his open mouth and never taking his eyes off the trapped frightened criminal .

Guided by the loud barks that resounded in the silent starry night, the police came running towards the pond, followed by George and some teachers.

"Good boy, what a hero. Good boy," the first policeman to arrive said to Buster, patting him affectionately on his solid side.

"And hello, hello," shouted the police sergeant as he ran up to the pond and looked down at the drowned kidnapper, "what do we have here? A sorry looking villain I believe."

Buster barked twice, as if in agreement with the police sergeant. The gangster was a sorry sight indeed.

"Let's be having him then lads," the sergeant shouted to his two men. "Drag that pitiful specimen outta that pond."

"You blooming dog! I'll get you one day!" the gangster screamed out as two policemen dragged him out and handcuffed him.

Buster cocked his head, wagged his tail, smiled his Staffy smile and whined. "Oooh oooh ooh" - meaning - "Serves you right, you nasty piece of work."

Then Buster panicked as he remembered his mum. His heart leapt again and he put his wagging tail between his legs and ran with his entire doggy might back to the school.

CHAPTER EIGHT
BUSTER IS FAMOUS

His mum was still sleeping. Doctor Bruce and the Secret Service man were also fast asleep. The ambulance paramedics were talking to the other teachers saying they thought they would be fine once the effects of the sleeping tablets wore off.

Buster listened to all this while he licked his mum's legs to help comfort her as the medics took her to the ambulance and onto hospital just to be sure she'd be ok. He whined and whined trying to wake her up and they had to lock the corridor door to stop him following her to the ambulance.

Leon was also feeling much better after his shock. The paramedics had checked him over and he was resting before the police came to interview him. His first thoughts after his rescue had been to come and thank his doggy friend when Buster returned. He shuffled over to Buster and gave the worried dog a huge hug to comfort him.

"Well done dude. What a brave dog you are. You saved my life and I'll never ever forget you Buster," he said rubbing Buster's white chest and cuddling his strong brown neck.

"He certainly did," the policewoman said, "and he saved that gangster's son's life too. He's been taken to hospital but the paramedics say he'll be ok once the doctors stitch his leg up and give him more blood. We all owe Buster more than he will ever know."

"I think Buster knows more than we all think," Zahra said hugging Buster. "He knew what was going to happen, that's why he tried to get to Bradley last night and why he disappeared to prevent his mum locking him in his room. He planned all this to protect us. He's cleverer than anyone knows."

"Well maybe he is my dear," the policewoman answered, giving Buster a pat. "Whatever he did, he saved the President of America's son's life and that is some tale we all will never forget."

Indeed, no one would forget what happened that night. Buster's mum, Dr Bruce and the guard all recovered the next day. The world's television and newspapers arrived and the American Secret Service and British police crawled all over the school and Bradley's father's house. They arrested the three kidnappers and many more of his father's evil gang.

Bradley was so sorry and ashamed of what he did. He told them all about the plot and helped them arrest them all. The police decided not to punish him and Bradley found a couple of lovely caring guardians to live with, well away from his father's gang's influences. Doctor Bruce even allowed him to come back to school once he was healed.

Everyone from the press and the government wanted to meet Buster but his Mum said no. She didn't want Buster to be distressed by too many flashing lights and noisy people and Doctor Bruce also said it was time his students got back to normal school life so he banned the press.

Buster didn't want any fuss too. All he wanted was to be with his Mum and his friends in the dormitory. Doctor Bruce now realised how happy the students were when he was with them and how much the dog meant to everyone and his stern heart melted.

"I have decided that Buster can have a new job," he told a delighted Miss Wood. He can be our therapy dog. He can attend classrooms and help those students who are like him, anxious and worried. Miss Wood, you have a good loving dog. Well, he is as long as we don't have any more dangerous people turn up. Then I'll be delighted if he turns angry and chases them off again. I 've had enough danger for a lifetime."

Miss Wood almost hugged her Headmaster, but one look at his fearsome face changed her mind, so she shook his hand and smiled. "Thank you so much sir. I guess Buster has also had enough danger for now ."

She and Buster left his office and the whole of the boarding house cheered them as they came back. "Three cheers for Buster and Miss Wood," Leon shouted out and all the kids cheered, "Hip, Hip, Hurray!"

Bradley returned one week later in time for the Speech Day. Leon came to his bedroom. Bradley was scared because he thought Leon would be angry. But Leon spoke gently to him. "Well Bradley, maybe now you will realise we all wanted to be your friend. We never knew how horrible your father had been to you. I am willing to let bygones be bygones if you'll just say sorry to everyone.... and of course, to Buster and Miss Wood."

Bradley dropped his head. He had learned a hard lesson and he really wanted to be one of the team not a loner so he looked at Leon and put out a hand and whispered. "I'm sorry Leon."

Leon shook his hand and smiled, "Come on buddy let's see the gang and you've got a big brown dog to hug."

So, that's how Bradley became friends with his fellow boarders and Buster. The happy hound licked him with his big tongue every time he saw him, comforting his wounded leg and followed him everywhere, watching over him like he did all his friends.

Buster thought nothing could be better than his life was now he could be with his friends.

But there was one more big surprise waiting for him

CHAPTER NINE
BUSTER GETS A SURPRISE

It was Speech Day. A huge marquee had been set up in the grounds for all the parents, staff and students to sit and listen to the dignitaries speak and receive the prizes for their efforts during the year. A lot of posh food and bubbly drinks were ready for afterwards for the parents but only soda for the kids. However, this Speech Day was going to be special. The main speaker was going to be Leon's mum - The President of the United States.

Doctor Bruce nearly collapsed when he heard. He was visited three days after the baddies were captured by three people in black suits and dark glasses with a well-dressed lady who told him they were Secret Service people and the American Ambassador to Great Britain. They told him that the President wanted to come to Speech Day and thank everyone for rescuing her son. His usual tough face went pale and he broke into a sweat as he wailed. "Oh, my Lord! How can we make that happen and what about my students and all the attention? She is so famous."

"You don't have to do anything Sir," the Ambassador said. "Our Secret Service and your police will keep everyone safe. We will arrange everything for her and your safety. She really wants to meet you all and give out the prizes and after the events that happened here, talk about friendship and forgiveness between all people."

And so, many men and women in black suits, earphones and sunglasses descended on the little country school to ensure everyone was safe from any other bad guys. The Head insisted he did not want the television and cameras in school and he got his way. Only school photographers would record what happened that special day.

The Headmaster was mildly annoyed when yet another helicopter landed on the playing field and a lot of Secret Service men surrounded the person who got out of it just before the speeches started.

"Who on earth is that now. No one told me another helicopter was coming. The President and the British politicians are already here. I'll be pleased when my school is back to normal."

He was still grumping when he went off to the marquee begin his opening speech.

The speeches and prize-giving went ahead as planned and everything was coming to an end. The President gave a wonderful speech about friendship between all countries and cultures, giving examples of the way school worked with so many different people and the recent kidnapping incident of how young people can pull together to help one another.

She was concluding her speech. "So, after all these prizes for special achievements to you wonderful students I'd like to give one more prize to a very, very special person who you all know very well. There's someone amongst us who I personally owe such a debt that I really cannot find the words to say."

She was handed a small box and she peered at the audience and continued. "Somewhere out there is our special friend, our school friend. He is not from a different country, or separate culture or colour but from a separate species and we love him as we do all our people...Buster where you are my dear boy?"

Miss Wood, who was sitting at the back of the marquee holding Buster on his lead, became faint as she heard the words. When she recovered, she stood up and shouted towards the President. "Here he is Miss!"

"Well bring the hero up. We all want to say thank you don't we folks?" the President said laughing and the whole audience stood up clapping loudly.

Kitty had never been as happy as when she walked her big brown, tail-wagging dog to the stage. She took him up the steps and they both met the most powerful person in the world who was smiling the loveliest smile. The President took a medal from the small case and she kneeled down facing Buster who licked her face, much to laughter of the audience. The President smiled and placed the medal's red, white and blue ribbon around Buster's neck and then she kissed the dog. Standing up she spoke into microphone.

"This is the Animals in War and Peace Medal of Bravery. It is the highest award for animal bravery we award in the United States, and Buster, I am proud to give it to you and to make you an honorary American."

Buster did not know why he had received this around his neck but he did know that the lady who had given him it was nice, like his mum. He also did not understand why all the people in the big tent were clapping but he knew they must be happy, so he smiled his special 'Staffy' smile as he wagged his tail continually.

His mum shook the President's hand and was turning to go back to her seat with Buster when the President touched her arm and said, "Don't go yet Miss Wood. My son has a special thank you present for you and his best friend Buster." And she turned and waved her son to come up stage from his seat in the audience.

Leon came up and Buster jumped up at him with joy. "Good boy dude," Leon said, stroking Buster. And grabbing Buster's medal hanging around the happy hound's neck, he showed it to the smiling crowd and shouted. "Well done Buster, our hero!" And all the parents clapped and the kids cheered.

Then, he took his mother's microphone and shouted out. "Now, how'd y'awl like to dance?"

And the school band began to play the introduction to Buster's favourite song.

Buster jumped up again at Leon to dance as they always did in the school common room but Leon pushed him playfully away laughing and shouted out. "Not with me dude. Why not with Beyoncé"

And he pointed to end of the stage. To the shock, amazement and joy of most of the audience (well, the parents were still wondering who Beyoncé was) from the side of the stage came the superstar. She took the microphone off Leon, the music stopped and she waved for the audience to stop clapping and whistling and spoke softly.

"Thanks Leon," and turning to the audience said, "welcome everyone it's great to be here in England." Everyone cheered.

"I see the Principal looks a bit shocked," she said looking and laughing at Doctor Bruce. "I'm sorry bro but Leon kept it secret from you all. He said the kids would love to see your face when I turn up to make Buster's day. He was right; you look as if you've seen a ghost. Chill out man, I've come at my friend Leon's request to thank a special dog. So, let's hear the music play" And she started to sing.

Leon took Buster by his two front paws and lifted him up on two legs and shouted down the microphone.

"Come on everyone let's celebrate and dance with Buster – the dog who danced with danger! "

Buster danced with Leon and his new found superstar singer on stage while everyone including a very happy Headmaster danced, clapped and sang. No one could hear the happy dog whining his own words to the song and no one would have understood anyway but he sang with joy....." oooh, oooh, oooh"

That night as he lay with his mum on her bed, his medal on his chest and the music in his head, he was the happiest dog in the world. He snuggled closer to her and put one leg over her tired body. He whined gently as he fell asleep.

"I love you Mum."

THE END

CHILDREN'S BOOKS BY DAVEY J. ASHFIELD

Buster: The Dog Who Danced With Danger
Tommy's Last Wish
Zahra's Christmas Wish